Fun Around Town

Peppa Pig™: Peppa's School Day (978-0-545-92547-1)
© Astley Baker Davies Ltd/Entertainment One UK Ltd 2003.
Peppa Pig™: Peppa Visits the Aquarium (978-1-338-05417-0)
© Astley Baker Davies Ltd/Entertainment One UK Ltd 2003.
Peppa Pig™: Daddy Pig's Old Chair (978-1-338-18305-4)
© Astley Baker Davies Ltd/Entertainment One UK Ltd 2003.
Peppa Pig™: Recycling Fun! (978-1-338-18326-9)
© Astley Baker Davies Ltd/Entertainment One UK Ltd 2003.

  ISBN 978-1-338-18622-2

10 9 8 7 6 5 4 3 2   17 18 19 20 21

Printed in China   38
First printing 2017

Contents

Peppa's School Day

Peppa's School Day

Adapted by Meredith Rusu

In this story, you will see:

Peppa

Suzy Sheep

slide

Madame Gazelle

Emily Elephant

building blocks

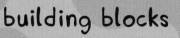

Peppa is going to school today.

All of her friends are there!

"Today we have a new student," says Madame Gazelle. "This is Emily Elephant."

Emily is shy.
She does not know what to say.

Everyone is excited to meet Emily!

"Can I show Emily how we do show-and-tell?" Peppa asks.

"Of course," says Madame
Gazelle.
Peppa tells the class about
her teddy bear.

Next, it is free time.

"What would you like to do today?" Peppa asks Emily.

There is painting, clay, or building blocks.

Emily chooses building blocks!

Peppa shows Emily how to stack the blocks.

"You put one on top of another," says Peppa.

"Like this?" asks Emily.
"Wow!" say the children.

Emily Elephant is good at stacking blocks!

Next, it is playtime!
"Come on, Emily," shouts
Peppa.

"At playtime, we go outside!"
says Candy Cat.

All the children run outside.

First, they go down the slide.

Wheeeee!

Then they play a game.
"Who is the loudest?" asks
Peppa. *Snort!*

They all make loud sounds.
What a lot of noise!

"Emily, you try," says Peppa.
Emily makes a noise like a
trumpet.

She is the loudest of all!

"Can you spin the hula hoop?" Suzy Sheep asks Emily.

Emily can spin the hula hoop.
She is good at lots of things!

But there is still one game
left to play.

"My favorite game is jumping in muddy puddles," says Peppa. "That is my favorite game, too!" shouts Emily.

Peppa and Emily are so happy
they are friends.
What a nice day at school!

Peppa Visits the Aquarium

Peppa Visits the Aquarium

Adapted by Meredith Rusu

In this story, you will see:

Peppa

George

Goldie

sea horses

Miss Rabbit

Candy Cat

aquarium

Every morning, Peppa gives
Goldie, her pet fish, breakfast.

"Time to eat!" she says.

Oh, dear.
Goldie is not eating.

"What is wrong with Goldie?"
Peppa asks.

"She looks a bit sad," says
Mummy Pig.

"I think she is lonely," says Peppa. "She doesn't have any fish friends."

"Maybe Goldie could visit the aquarium," says Daddy Pig.

"What is the aquarium?"
Peppa asks.

"It is a place with lots of fish," says Daddy Pig.

"Oh, goodie!" cries Peppa.
"We can find a friend for
Goldie there. Let's go!"

Peppa and her family drive to the aquarium.
Beep, beep!

Miss Rabbit sells them
tickets.
  "The fish can go in for free!"
she says. "Enjoy your visit!"

The first room has many little fish.

"Could one of these fish be Goldie's new friend?" asks Daddy Pig.

"No," says Peppa. "They are too small."

Peppa's friend, Candy Cat, is in the next room with her family.

"Hello, Candy!" says Peppa.
"We are finding a friend for
Goldie."

The fish in this room look
like little dinosaurs.
"Dine-saw!" says George.
"These aren't dinosaurs," says
Candy. "They are called sea
horses."

"Could a sea horse be Goldie's friend?" Candy asks.

"No," says Peppa. "They are too dinosaur-y."

Everyone goes to
the next room.

The tank in here has a very strange fish.

"Wow!" says Daddy Pig. "This fish looks like a big eye!"

It is a big eye . . . on a very
BIG fish!
"Maybe this one could be
Goldie's new friend!" says
Mummy Pig.

"No," says Peppa. "It is TOO big!"
Glub, glub!

There is only one room left to visit.
   But there are no fish in this tank. There is only green slime.

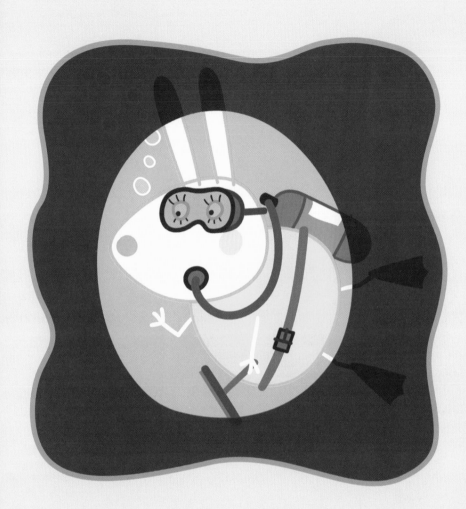

Oh! And Miss Rabbit is in the tank, too.
She is cleaning it.

The last stop is the café.
"We did not find a friend for
Goldie," Peppa says sadly.
Then, Peppa notices a bowl on
the counter.

"What is that?" Peppa asks.
"This is my pet goldfish,
Ginger," says Miss Rabbit.

Goldie likes Ginger.
Ginger likes Goldie.

"Goldie can visit Ginger any time she wants," says Miss Rabbit.

Glub, glub!
Hee, hee!
Goldie has made a friend at the aquarium after all.

Daddy Pig's Old Chair

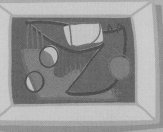

Daddy Pig's
Old Chair

Adapted by Ellen Philpott

In this story, you will see:

chair

Peppa

Madame Gazelle

Daddy Pig

Mummy Pig

rummage sale

"We have to buy
a new school roof,"
says Madame Gazelle.
"We will have a rummage
sale to make money."

Peppa gives her toys to the
rummage sale, to make money.

"I will give this toy, too,"
says Peppa.

"You can give this old chair, Daddy," says Peppa.

"No. This is a very good chair," says Daddy Pig.

Peppa gives all the toys
to Madame Gazelle.

"You can have this old chair, too,"
says Mummy Pig.

Peppa, Mummy Pig, and Daddy Pig go to the rummage sale. Peppa's friends go, too.

Daddy's chair is at the rummage sale. It looks very old.

Peppa looks at all the toys with her friends. Her old toy looks very good.

"I will buy my old toy back," says Peppa.

All her friends buy their old toys back, too.

"I will buy this chair," says
Daddy. "It will look good with
the old one."

"No. It IS the old one!"
says Mummy Pig.

"Oh. It was a lot of money," says
Daddy Pig.

"Good," says Madame Gazelle.
"We have made
a lot of money. We can
buy a new school roof!"

Peppa is glad buying her toy back helped her school. And Daddy Pig is glad he has his chair back!

Recycling Fun

Adapted by Lorraine Horsley

In this story, you will see:

Mummy Pig

Peppa

George

car

Daddy Pig

truck

Mr. Bull

newspapers

bottles

cans

Miss Rabbit

Mr. Bull is collecting
trash.

Mr. Bull puts the trash in the back of his truck.

Peppa, George, and
Mummy Pig are
collecting trash, too.

They collect bottles,
cans, and newspapers.

"We can recycle much of this trash," says Mummy Pig.

They put the trash
in the car.

Mummy Pig has
all the bottles.

Peppa has all the cans.

George has all the newspapers.

Miss Rabbit is recycling
trash, too. She is
recycling cars.

Daddy Pig recycles the
bottles.

Mummy Pig and Peppa recycle the cans.

"I like this!" Peppa says.

George recycles the
newspapers.

Oh no! Miss Rabbit is recycling Daddy Pig's car!

"Stop!" says Daddy Pig. "Stop! That is not recycling! That is our car!"

"Oh," says Miss Rabbit.
"I like recycling too much!"

"Our car is not trash," says
Daddy Pig.

"No," says Peppa.
"We like our car!"